Can you whistle, Johanna?

Can you whistle, Johanna?

ULF STARK
ANNA HÖGLUND

GECKO PRESS

One afternoon when Berra and I were
bouncing up and down on our homemade
seesaw, I told him that I was going to
visit my grandfather to eat cake, because
it was his birthday.

"And then he'll give me five dollars," I said.

"Does he give you money when it's his birthday?" asked Berra.

"Yep," I said. "He gives me money every time I see him."

"Wow. He must be all right then," said Berra.

"He is," I said. "And then I'll give him a big cigar."

Berra looked up at the clouds longingly. "I wish I had a grandfather too," he mumbled. "What do they do exactly?"

"They take you out to tea," I said. "And they eat pigs' trotters."

"You're joking," said Berra.

"No, it's true," I said. "Pigs' trotters in jelly. And sometimes they take you to a lake to catch fish."

"Why don't I have a grandfather?" Berra wondered.

"I don't know," I said. "But I do know where you can get one."

"Where's that?" asked Berra.

"I'll tell you tomorrow," I said. "I'd better go now. I have to put on a white shirt and comb my hair."

When I jumped off the seesaw, Berra shot down and hit his chin.

OUCH!

The next day I took Berra with me.

　　He had washed. He'd covered the cut
on his chin and he was carrying a marigold
he'd found in Mr. Gustavsson's garden.

"Do I look all right?" he asked.

I nodded, because you don't often see him looking so clean.

We went past the bakery and its warm toasty smells, and past a clump of trees where the birds always sing. Then we carried on past the chapel where the hearses are usually parked, shiny in the sun.

And then we were almost there.

"There," I said. "That's where you can find your grandfather. There are lots of old men in there."

I pointed to the old people's home.

★　★　★

We wandered down a dark corridor with
pictures on the walls and we kept going
the whole way along till we came to a
door that was slightly open.

"Let's have a look in there," I whispered
to Berra.

An old man was sitting inside,
playing cards at a table.

"That's him!" I whispered in Berra's
red ear. "He looks old enough, don't
you think?"

"Yes," said Berra when he had looked at him for a moment. "But I've changed my mind anyhow."

"You can't," I said. "You have to at least go in and say hello!"

So Berra went in.

"Good afternoon!" he called out. "Pardon me, but do you like to eat pigs' trotters?"

"Whassat you say?" said the old man, turning around so we could see that he also had a cut on his chin. "Do I eat pigs' trotters? No, I'm playing a game of patience. Who are you?"

"My name is Berra," said Berra. "I've come to visit. I've brought you a flower."

He held out the marigold he'd been hiding behind his back. It was yellow and it looked a bit warm.

"That's very nice of you." The old man smiled. "Won't you come in?"

We went in and Berra held out his flower again. "Here you are, Grandpa!" he said.

The old man looked first at the flower and then at Berra. He scratched his thin, white hair.

"What's this?" he said. "Am I your grandfather?"

"That's right." Berra smiled. "I'm here at last. It hasn't really been sort of possible to come any earlier."

The old man gave Berra a hug.

"Well, my, but how you've grown," he said, rubbing his eyes with his knuckles. "How old are you now?"

"Seven," said Berra.

"Seven!" said the old man. "There I was, just sitting and feeling a bit lonely, and then you came along!"

"That's right," Berra agreed.

"But who is this?" the old man asked, nodding towards me. "I'm not his grandfather as well, am I?"

Berra laughed so hard that you could see where he'd lost his front teeth.

"No," he said. "That's Ulf and he's already got one."

"And my name is Ned," said the old man, taking me by the hand.

Then he showed us his room.

There was a photograph of a woman with big eyes and a hat. There was a gold clock, a stuffed bird and half a moose he'd carved out of wood.

"That's all there is to see," he sighed. "What shall we do now? There isn't much to do in here."

"Ulf's grandfather usually takes him out to afternoon tea," said Berra.

"That's a good idea," said the old man whose name was Ned, and who had just become Berra's grandfather. "I'll just get my stick."

* * *

The cafeteria in the old people's home was full of old ladies and old men.

We sipped our tea and nibbled at the cakes we'd been given and I explained about my grandfather and how it was his birthday. Suddenly the old man grabbed hold of Berra and lifted him up onto the table. He banged his teacup with a teaspoon till the room went absolutely quiet.

"THIS BOY HERE IS MY GRANDSON!" he called out proudly. "HIS NAME IS BERRA AND TODAY HE HAS GIVEN ME A MARIGOLD."

Berra went as red in the face as the rest home's table napkins. When he climbed down from the table, an old lady called Tora came up closer to have a look at him.

"Ooh Ned, he looks just like you," she said.

"That's right, because we both have cuts on our chins," said Berra.

The old lady was about to pat him on the head when the old man poked her with his stick.

"This is my grandson!" he yelled. "You leave him alone!"

*　*　*

Back in the old man's room, Berra took his hand.

"Goodbye then, Grandpa," he said. "This was really fun!"

"Yes, I enjoyed your visit," said Grandpa Ned.

He stood in the doorway watching us as we went.

After a while Berra stopped.

"Grandpa, there's just one thing I forgot," he said.

"Is that right?" said the old man. "What have you forgotten?"

"Well, it's just that usually when you visit your grandfather, you get given some money. Ulf always does."

"How much does he get, usually?" wondered Grandpa Ned.

"Sometimes two dollars," I said. "If it's a special occasion, then I get five."

"Well then, let's make it five for today," said Grandpa Ned, hunting in his pocket for his wallet.

Berra was very pleased with his new grandfather. The whole way home he hopped and jumped and threw his coins up in the air.

The next day he wanted to go again, even though it was raining so hard that our hair got wet.

Grandpa Ned seemed pleased with Berra too. He rubbed his hair with a towel for a long time after we arrived.

"I almost thought you were a dream," he said.

Berra pinched Grandpa Ned in the leg so he could feel that he was awake. Then we played cards. We listened to the rain clattering against the window, and the old man passed us the picture of the woman with the big eyes so we could look at it more closely.

"That is my wife," he said. "Well, shall we go and have some afternoon tea now?"

"I don't know," said Berra. "Ulf's grandfather usually takes him to a lake so they can catch fish."

"Is that right," sighed the old man.

He put the picture of his wife back. Then he looked at the raindrops running down the windowpane.

"I can't do that," he said, after a while.
"I can't walk that far. I just get lost.
And I don't know where to find a lake."

"It doesn't matter," I said. "We usually
only catch tiddlers."

"And cakes taste better anyway,"
said Berra.

So off we went to afternoon tea.
Tora stroked the old man on the chin
and pinched Berra's cheeks when Ned
wasn't looking.

When we were ready to go, Ned gave
Berra two dollars and he gave me a mint.

"I'm sorry about the fishing," he said.

"But I'm sure I can think of something else."

"Like what?" Berra wondered.

"You never know," said the old man.

*　*　*

Several weeks passed before he'd thought of something else. But one day, when we came to his room, he had his coat on.

"Okay boys, now we are going out!" he clucked, pleased with himself.

We had to help him tie his shoelaces. Berra got to carry the bag he'd packed.

We went out into the park. Grandpa Ned stopped and blinked at the sun shining high over the big chimney above the old people's home.

"I had almost forgotten it was like this," he said.

"Like what?" wondered Berra.

"Can you hear the birds?" the old man asked.

"Yes," we answered.

"Can you smell all the smells?" he asked.

"Yes, of course we can," said Berra.

"Never forget it," he said.

We kept going. We went past the place where they keep all the wheelchairs. We sneaked past Tora, who was sitting on a seat feeding sparrows. And then we stopped at a park bench.

"Let's see what we have here," said Grandpa Ned, opening his bag.

He brought out the things he had in the bag. There was a pair of scissors, a knife with a red handle, a fishing line, some string, a needle and thread. Last of all he took something right out of the bottom of the bag.

It was a scarf with roses on it, made from material that was thin and shiny.

"I gave this to my wife once," he said. "Can you feel how soft it is?"

We felt how soft it was.

"And can you feel how light it is?" he asked with pleasure.

We weighed it in our hands.
It weighed almost nothing.

"It is real silk," said Grandpa Ned. "Silk is the most beautiful material there is. It's the best thing to use if you want to make a kite."

"Are we going to make a kite?" cried Berra.

So we built a kite out of sticks we found
in the bushes.

Grandpa Ned stretched the material over the sticks and sewed it in place exactly where it should be.

The birds sang in the trees. And the old man whistled as well. He was whistling a beautiful tune called "Can you whistle, Johanna?"

"My wife's name was Johanna," he told us.

Then he talked about his wife, who had red hair and a blue hat, and Berra said that he would like to learn to whistle, too. After a while the old man held up the kite.

"Now it's ready," he said, pleased.
"What do you think?"

"It doesn't have a tail!" said Berra.

The old man took off his tie.

"It can have my tie," he said.

There never was a more beautiful kite!

The only thing was that it couldn't fly, because there wasn't any wind. It didn't matter how much we ran and threw it up into the sky.

"You'll have to fly it another day," said the old man. "I must go home now and rest a bit."

And he picked up his bag and went off, in completely the wrong direction.

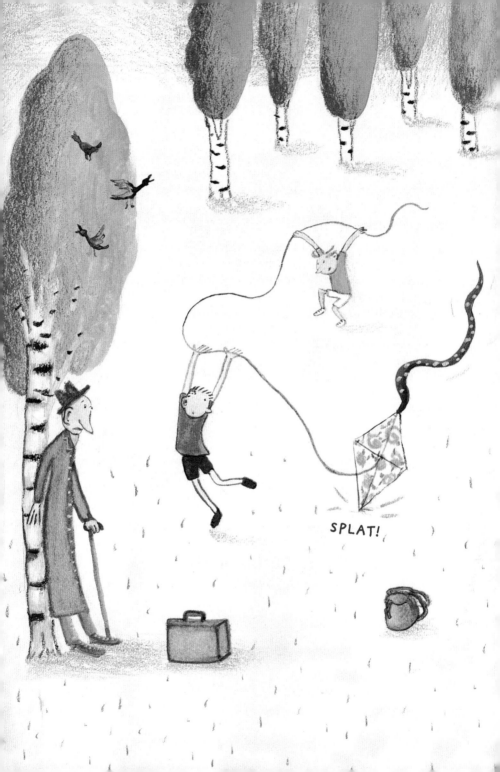

SPLAT!

Tick tock
tick tock

The next time we visited Ned, he was in bed. He had a glass of water beside him, and a vase with the marigold, which had lost its petals.

"Have you made the kite fly yet?" he asked.

"No, we've been waiting for the wind," said Berra. "And here you are, all tucked up in bed."

"I just wanted to think about things a bit today," said Grandpa Ned.

We sat on the end of the bed while he was thinking. We looked at the stuffed bird and the gold clock. And we didn't say a word for at least five minutes.

"I think about things a lot too," Berra said after a while.

"Is that right, and what do you think about, then?" asked the old man.

"About what you liked doing best when you were young," said Berra.

Grandpa Ned had to think about that for quite a while. He rubbed his chin, which now had two cuts on it.

"Well," he said. "Stealing cherries was probably what I liked doing best, because it was so exciting—and because they tasted so good."

"Personally, I would like to learn how to whistle," said Berra.

So the old man showed Berra how. He showed him what shape to make his mouth and how he should hold his tongue.

"Now all you have to do is blow,"
he said. "Like this."

He whistled "Can you whistle,
Johanna?" But when Berra tried,
all he could manage was a hoarse
little hissing sound.

"This doesn't work at all," he complained.

"Yes it does," said Grandpa Ned.
"You just have to keep trying, otherwise
nothing will happen."

He looked at Berra. "Is there anything
else you are thinking about?"

"Yes," said Berra. "About why you
always have a cut on your chin."

"It happens when I shave myself,"
said Ned. "It's because my hands shake
so much."

"Then you will have to stop doing it," said Berra. "Ulf can shave you. He is good at carving wood." He swung his legs a bit. "There's just one more thing."

"Is that right, and what is that?" asked the old man.

"I want to know when your birthday is," said Berra. "Usually you do something for your grandfather when it's his birthday."

Grandpa Ned looked at the gold clock hanging on the wall.

"I think it will have to be soon," he said.

"Maybe next Friday?" said Berra.

"Yes, maybe so," the old man answered.

* * *

We only stayed a little while longer, because Berra had a lot of things he had to do.

He had to check his batteries. He had to smash his piggy bank. And because there wasn't a lot of money in it, we had to cut three people's lawns and weed Mr. Gustavsson's rose bed.

The whole time, Berra kept trying to whistle.

He tried on Wednesday when we went to the tobacconist to buy the biggest cigar I had ever seen.

He tried on Thursday when we went together to Timgren's Supermarket, the bakery and another shop that was quite expensive.

Even on Friday, while he was packing his backpack, Berra blew till his cheeks were round and red as two half tomatoes. And still he didn't whistle a single note.

"This is hard work," said Berra when we went past the little chapel. "This is the hardest thing I haven't learned in my whole life."

When we got to Grandpa Ned that Friday it had already started to get dark.

He was sitting on a chair in the middle of the room. He had on his best suit and his chin was full of stubble.

"Ah ha, so you came after all," he said. "I was starting to think you had forgotten me."

"We won't ever do that," said Berra. "HAPPY BIRTHDAY, GRANDPA!"

"Happy Birthday, Grandpa Ned," I said.

And after we had sung "Happy Birthday" it was time to shave him.

Berra soaped his chin with a brush till it looked like a cream cake. And I drew a shaving knife carefully over his skin so it was as smooth and soft as the silk of our kite.

"There you go," said Berra when we had dried him off with a damp towel. "Now the party can begin!"

"They will have closed the cafeteria now," said Grandpa Ned gloomily.

"Bound to have," I said.

"But what does it matter!" said Berra. "Tonight we are going to eat out!"

In the corridor we passed a nurse in a pale uniform. She looked at the old man's brown hat.

"And where is Ned off to?" she asked.

"I am going to a party with my grandson and his best friend," said the old man. "It's my birthday today, you see."

"I didn't know that," she said.

"No, it's a secret," said Berra.

The nurse gave Ned a pat on the back. "Happy Birthday!" she said. "Have a nice time. Be careful of his heart, boys. It's not so good."

Berra gave her a look. "It's the best heart there is," he said.

And off we went out into the park where there were a thousand smells and swallows were swishing in the air.

"What shall we do now?" Grandpa Ned wondered. "Shall we eat now?"

"No, first we have to do something really fun," said Berra.

"That's right. And exciting," I said.

We went to Mr. Gustavsson's garden. It was so dark that Berra had to use his light.

"You'll have to be very quiet now, Grandpa," whispered Berra.

"I'll do my best," the old man promised.

"Good," I said. "Because Gustavsson is the worst of everybody."

We crept past the flagpole, past the gooseberry bush and a window with light shining from it. And then we stopped.

"Here!" said Berra. "Here it is!"

He shone the light up the trunk of Mr. Gustavsson's enormous cherry tree. And up in the sky we could glimpse heavy clusters of ripe cherries.

"Let's climb," said Berra.

But Grandpa Ned shook his head. "I can't," he said.

"Of course you can," said Berra. "You just have to keep trying, otherwise nothing will happen."

"And there are branches the whole way up," I said.

The old man leaned his stick against the tree. Then he started to climb. He went very slowly. He grabbed hold of branches with his shaky hands. After a while he stopped, because he couldn't get his foot up to the next branch.

"Do you want to come down again?" I asked.

"Not on your life!" The old man giggled. "Just give me a leg up, boy!"

At last, we were all sitting side by side in the tree, Grandpa Ned dangling his legs like a small boy.

"I did it!" he chuckled. "Did you see me?"

"Yes," said Berra. "Ulf's grandfather would never have managed that."

"You're right," I admitted. "He'd never manage that."

"Ah," said the old man. "Ah well." He looked up through the leaves. "Well, now it's time to pick cherries!"

He took off his hat. We filled it with the biggest and juiciest cherries we could find. We sat quietly and just enjoyed eating them.

We looked out over the world and spat our cherry stones on the ground. And Grandpa Ned didn't want to leave.

"Here we are sitting, just like in heaven," he said, taking the last red cherry out of his hat.

Berra and I were already back on the ground as Grandpa Ned slowly climbed down. He waved proudly with his brown hat.

"Wow, what a grandfather!" said Berra.

"Yeah, but mine's better at fishing," I said.

We saw Grandpa Ned put his foot on the bottom branch. And then we heard the crack as it broke off.

When we got to him, he was lying absolutely still.

"Are you all right, Grandpa?" Berra asked.

"Quite all right," said the old man. "I just need to rest for a bit."

Then we heard the door to Mr. Gustavsson's house opening.

"Cripes!" said Berra. "We'll have to hurry."

"This is where it gets exciting," I said.

We all hid behind a bush just as Mr. Gustavsson came striding out over the grass. He stopped at the cherry tree. He looked at the branch that had broken off and he saw the cherry stones on the ground.

"JUST YOU WAIT!" he yelled. "JUST YOU WAIT TILL I GET HOLD OF YOU LITTLE BRATS!"

The old man started to giggle.

He giggled so much that Berra had to put his hand over his mouth. He was still giggling when Gustavsson gave up and we went off to get on with our party.

We went to the clump of trees behind
the chapel.

Berra laid out everything he had with
him in his backpack. There was a thermos
of tea. There were cakes from the bakery
and pigs' trotters in jelly that we'd bought
from Timgren's Supermarket.

Berra lit the candles and placed them
here and there on the ground.

"Please start," he said.

Grandpa Ned ate some of the cakes
and drank his tea as the stars came out
like daisies in the sky. He asked if we
had flown the kite yet. And we told
him there still hadn't been any wind.
At last the old man wiped his mouth.

"Would you like some pigs' trotters
now perhaps?" asked Berra.

The old man looked at the flabby lumps.

"They're in jelly," I said. "My grandfather
loves them."

"I'm afraid I don't," said Grandpa Ned.

"I bet no one does in our family,"
said Berra. "But you like cigars, don't you?"

"Yes, I love cigars," said the old man.

We took out the cigar. Grandpa Ned
lit it and sent small clouds of smoke
puffing towards the sky.

"The cigar is from both of us,"
said Berra. "But this is just from me."

He held out a parcel tied up with
paper and string.

When Grandpa Ned had taken off the paper, he could see that it was a tie.

"It's made of real silk," said Berra. "That's why it was so incredibly expensive."

Ned looked at the tie. He didn't say anything for a long time. He just kept coughing because he'd got smoke in his lungs.

"Imagine me getting a grandson like you," he said.

"Yeah, and me getting a grandfather like you," said Berra.

When it was time for us to go home, Grandpa Ned was too tired to walk. I had to go and get a wheelchair from the old people's home. He sat in it, whistling, as we pushed it past the chapel.

"Well, have you learned to whistle yet?" he asked Berra.

"Not really," said Berra.

"Next time you visit I'd like to hear you whistle," said Grandpa Ned.

"Okay, you will," said Berra. "I promise."

After that evening it was a while before I saw Berra again.

But one afternoon I found him behind a tree. He was sitting there trying to make his mouth into a trumpet.

"Do you want to go and visit Grandpa Ned again soon?" I asked.

"Nah, I have to learn to whistle first," he said.

He blew up his cheeks. I went on my way. I knew he wanted to work on it on his own.

It took several weeks.

★　★　★

But one day when the air was cooler
and the leaves on Mr. Gustavsson's
cherry tree had started to turn yellow,
Berra turned up. His eyes were tired
but happy and he punched me lightly
in the stomach.

"Now we can go to see Grandpa,"
he said.

He ran the whole way.

He ran right up to the old man's door.

"I'm here now!" he called out as he opened it.

But when we looked in, Grandpa Ned wasn't there, and neither was the gold clock, the stuffed bird nor the picture of the woman with the blue hat.

The bed was made. And the room smelled of soap.

"That's strange," I said. "Maybe he's in the park."

In the park we could hear the birds singing. We could smell all the smells. But we couldn't find Grandpa Ned.

So we went to the cafeteria, where Tora saw us.

"Would you like some tea, boys?" she asked.

"No," said Berra. "We're looking for Grandpa."

The old lady got up. She wiped her mouth with her napkin. Then she put her hand on Berra's shoulder.

"He is not here any more," she said. "He has left us."

"He's probably got lost," said Berra. "He always does."

Tora put her arm around Berra's shoulders. She told him that his grandfather was up in heaven now. She said that we should say goodbye to him in the chapel on Saturday.

Berra was so angry that he got tears in his eyes. He pulled himself out of the old lady's arms.

"And I've learned how to whistle and everything," he cried.

He didn't say a word the whole way home.

He just kept kicking at stones.

On Saturday the wind came.
The leaves rustled and white clouds
were sailing across the sky when
Berra came to my house.

He was wearing his good shirt
and his spiky hair was combed down
with water.

"Now we can go and say goodbye
to Grandpa," he said.

But first we went through
Mr. Gustavsson's garden and picked
his most beautiful rose.

There was a hearse outside the chapel.
Inside, the ceremony had already started.
An old man was playing the organ as
hard as he could. Tora was there in black
clothes, as well as a nurse and some
other people, all looking at the white
coffin in the middle of the room.

"Let's sit down here," said Berra.
"You get a good view from here."

We sat down on the bench closest
to the door.

When the music was quiet, a priest came
out and made a speech. It was quite short.

"Ned was a happy man. Especially at the end," he said. "We all liked him. So he was never alone, even though he didn't have any relatives."

Berra stuck up his hand. He waved it so everybody looked at him.

"But he did," he said. "He was my grandpa."

After that everybody went up and put flowers on the coffin.

Berra and I went last. We bowed our heads. Berra put Mr. Gustavsson's rose on top of the others.

He still stood there, even when I pulled him by the arm.

"Listen to this!" he said. "I can whistle now!"

And then Berra whistled so it echoed all around the chapel. He whistled "Can you whistle, Johanna?"

*   *   *

"How did that sound?" he asked when we came outside.

"Really good," I said. "You should be pleased."

"I am pleased," said Berra.

We stood in the wind and watched the coffin being put in the hearse by a couple of old men wearing black gloves.

"We had fun with Grandpa Ned, anyway," said Berra.

And then the hearse drove off.
We waved to it until it disappeared
around the corner.

"What shall we do now?" I asked.

"Let's go fly the kite," said Berra.
"Because today the wind is blowing."

This edition first published in 2021 by Gecko Press
PO Box 9335, Wellington 6141, New Zealand
info@geckopress.com

English-language edition © Gecko Press Ltd 2005, 2021
Translation © Julia Marshall 2005
Text © Ulf Stark 1992
Illustrations © Anna Höglund 1992
First published by Bonnier Carlsen Bokförlaget, Stockholm, Sweden
Published in the English language by arrangement with Bonnier Group Agency, Stockholm, Sweden

Distributed in the United States and Canada by Lerner Publishing Group, lernerbooks.com
Distributed in the United Kingdom by Bounce Sales and Marketing, bouncemarketing.co.uk
Distributed in Australia and New Zealand by Walker Books Australia, walkerbooks.com.au

Design and typesetting by Vida & Luke Kelly Design
Printed in China by Everbest Printing Co. Ltd, an accredited ISO 14001 & FSC-certified printer

ISBN hardback: 978-1-77657-325-7
ISBN paperback: 978-1-77657-326-4
Ebook available

For more curiously good books, visit geckopress.com